ISBN 0-590-54425-X

Text copyright © 1995 Nancy Hall, Inc.
Illustrations copyright © 1995 Carolyn Croll.
All rights reserved. Published by Scholastic Inc.
CARTWHEEL BOOKS and the CARTWHEEL BOOKS logo
are registered trademarks of Scholastic Inc.

12  11  10  9  8  7  6  5  4  3  2  1          5  6  7  8  9/9  0/0

Printed and assembled in Singapore. Necklace made in China.
First Scholastic printing, November 1995

# LITTLE STAR

Text by Mary Packard

Illustrations by Carolyn Croll

Book design by Antler & Baldwin Design Group

◆

SCHOLASTIC INC.

New York   Toronto   London   Auckland   Sydney

Long, long ago, when man, woman, earth, and sky still spoke the language of the spirits, a Lakota chief named Iron Horse lived with his wife, Laughing Cloud, in a peaceful village on the prairie. They had been childless for many years.

One night, when the sky was alive with stars, Laughing Cloud chose the smallest one to wish upon.

Her heart leaped with joy as she watched the tiny star tumble from the sky, for—as every Lakota woman knew—a falling star was the sign that a child would be born!

And sure enough, when nine moons had come and gone, the people welcomed a new life into their village! Chief Iron Horse and Laughing Cloud named their daughter Little Star, in honor of the Great Star Spirit, who had blessed their baby's birth.

As the seasons passed, Little Star grew to be a lovely young girl, who was known for her kindness as well as her beauty.

One day Grandmother Gray Feather presented the child with a beaded necklace that she had made herself. In its center was a little star.

"Keep this with you always, Little Star," she said, "and your fondest wish will come true. Just remember to make your wish wisely," added Grandmother. "Do not waste it, for there may come a day when you will need it."

Little Star wore her necklace always. She wore it as she tracked lizards through the tall grasses. She wore it when she carried her doll in its cradle board, and even when she played hoops and poles, a game that she loved.

But even more than dolls and games, Little Star loved horses—their gentle eyes, soft noses, and the eager way they greeted her.

She led them to the river for long, cool drinks. She brought them to where the sweetest grasses grew. She brushed their tails and combed their manes and rode them bareback over the prairie.

Each night before she went to bed, Little Star would play a special game with her mother.

"Do you know how much I would like a horse of my own?" she would ask.

And each night, Laughing Cloud would say, "Tell me, Little Star."

Little Star would think and think. If only she could make her mother understand.

"More than a basketful of berries in winter," the child would answer, "or a tepee filled with breezes on a hot summer's day."

"You will have a horse of your own, when the time is right," Laughing Cloud would always reply.

After she helped her father tend the horses, Little Star would often ask, "Is it time for me to get a horse of my own, Father?"

But Chief Iron Horse would always reply, "Not yet, Little Star. There is more to life than tending horses. A little girl must learn how to cook, sew, and do beadwork."

It was at times such as these that Little Star would be tempted to use up her wish and get a horse of her own. But then she would always think better of it.

"I'll save my wish in case I really need it," she would decide.

Little Star learned how to prepare wild rice, buffalo stew, and little cakes made out of corn flour. When her lessons were over, she would always save a portion to share with the horses in the pasture. Her favorite, Swift Eagle, was especially glad to get these tasty treats, and was always the first to greet her with a grateful whinny.

Little Star learned to sew and do beadwork. She made
buckskin leggings and moccasins for herself and several
saddle blankets to keep the horses warm in winter.

When she was through with her beading, instead of wearing her work as the other girls did, she would weave the colorful strands through Swift Eagle's mane and hang them from her bridle.

One evening, before she went to bed, Little Star walked out to the pasture to say good night to the horses. As usual, as soon as they spotted her, they trotted toward her eagerly, tossing their heads in greeting. But something was wrong. Swift Eagle was not among them!

Little Star searched and searched. It wasn't long before she heard a cry. She followed the sound until she came to a patch of tall grass. In the center of it lay Swift Eagle, moaning in pain. Little Star knelt down to comfort her.

"I'm going for help," she murmured in her ear. "Father will make you better. You'll see."

Little Star returned with Chief Iron Horse.  One look at the mare told him what was bothering her.

"If all goes well, by morning Swift Eagle will be a mother," he said.  "I'm sure your mother will not object if you stay up to watch the birth," he added.

How happy Little Star was to hear this news! Soon there would be another horse in the pasture—a baby horse for her to play with and to love.

But as the night wore on, Chief Iron Horse's smile became a deep frown. Something was terribly wrong. Swift Eagle was getting weaker. Her head lay still and her eyelids drooped wearily. It appeared that she might give up.

"Please help her," Little Star begged her father.

Chief Iron Horse shook his head sadly. "I'm afraid that only the spirits can help her now."

Tears filled Little Star's eyes. The pasture would seem so empty without Swift Eagle! Then she remembered Grandmother Gray Feather's words: "Save your wish, Little Star, for the day may come when you need it."

The day had come! Little Star pressed her necklace to her heart and said in a clear, strong voice, "Here is my wish: Please let Swift Eagle and her baby live."

Chief Iron Horse watched in wonder as, little by little, Swift Eagle seemed to gain back her strength. Her eyes became brighter and her breathing stronger. Then just as dawn was lighting up the eastern sky and the morning star shone down upon them, the foal was born at last!

"How tiny she is!" squealed Little Star.

"And perfectly formed," added her father. "Did you notice the mark on her face?"

Little Star's heart skipped a beat as the foal slowly turned its head toward her. Right in the center of its forehead was a star!

"I am proud of you, Little Star," said Chief Iron Horse.
"Your special wish was for another, not for yourself. Now
I know that you are ready to have a horse of your own.
And I can see," he added, pointing to the star on the foal's
forehead, "that this one was meant especially for you."

Little Star thought her heart would burst! Hugging her foal gently, she said, "I will take care of you always."

Little Star named her foal Morning Star, after the star that shone on the morning of her birth. The young horse grew to be as strong and swift as her mother before her, and the little girl and her horse became a familiar sight as they streaked through the tall grasses, fast as the wind. All who saw them agreed that Little Star and Morning Star were the brightest stars on the prairie.